THE PRINCE OF THE DOLOMITES

The Prince
of the
Dolomites

AN OLD ITALIAN TALE RETOLD AND ILLUSTRATED BY

Tomie de Paola

HARCOURT BRACE JOVANOVICH · NEW YORK AND LONDON

FOR TRINA AND BOB,

WHOM I LOVE VERY MUCH

Requests for permission to make copies of any part of the work should be mailed to:
Permissions, Harcourt Brace Jovanovich, Inc., 757 Third Avenue, New York, New York 10017

Printed in the United States of America

Library of Congress Cataloging in Publication Data
De Paola, Thomas Anthony.   Prince of the Dolomites.
Summary: Because of the love of Prince Pazzo of the Dolomites for Princess Lucia of the Moon,
the black peaks of the Dolomite mountains are changed to glimmering white, blue, pink, and yellow.
[1. Folklore—Italy]   I. Title.   PZ8.1.D43Pr   398.2′1′0945 [E]   79-18524
ISBN 0-15-263528-9   ISBN 0-15-674432-5 pbk.
First edition   B C D E

"He's coming, he's coming," the boy shouted as he ran
through the streets of the little Italian village.
"Zio Narratore is coming. Hurry!"

The children tumbled out of their houses
and ran down the road.

And there indeed was Uncle Storyteller climbing the hill.
In a moment, he was surrounded by the children, who hung
on his sleeves and thrust gifts of fruit, bread, and cheese
into his arms.

"Tell us a story, Uncle," they cried.
"We've waited and waited for you."

"Ah, *ragazzini,* I am here," the old storyteller said,
wiping his brow with a large handkerchief.
"*Grazie.* Thank you. What a fine lunch
you've brought me!"

He took his time finding a place to sit.
Then he patted a few heads, pinched a few cheeks,
ate a few things,
and drank a long drink from his wineskin.
The children waited.

He knew not to start too soon.

"So you want Zio Narratore to tell you a story, eh?"
the old man said at last.

"Yes! Yes!" the children shouted.

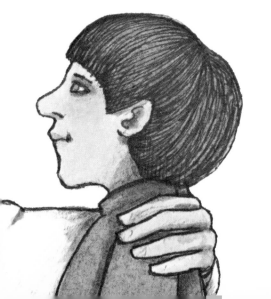

"Well . . . I do have a story," Uncle Storyteller said,
pointing to the gleaming pink, white, and blue mountains
that surrounded the little village in the Italian Alps.

"Did you know that our beautiful Dolomites were not always
so gleaming bright? Once—a long, long time ago—
before most people can remember, they were dark
and somber-looking mountains. They were so dark
that they seemed to keep the very sun from the valley."

"How did they become so bright?" asked one child.
"How could they change so much?"
"Was it because of the sun?" asked another.

"Aha," said Zio Narratore with a smile. "It was not the sun,
but the *moon* that made them bright."

"The MOON?" shouted the children. "How could the moon—"

"And," interrupted Zio, his voice becoming softer,
"they were changed by the most powerful force we know—
by love."

Zio Narratore pointed again
to the beautiful Dolomite mountains, shining in the sun.

Then he began.

In ancient times...

when the Dolomites were dark,
this land was ruled over
by a fine and just queen,
who was also a widow.

Her husband, the king, much loved
by his people, had been killed
in a hunting accident only days
after the queen had given birth
to their first and only child.

The king had held his son but once.

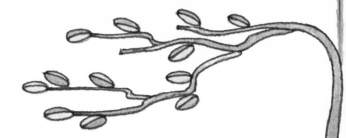

The boy grew and was as kind
and good as his father.
He spread happiness everywhere he went.
His smile lighted up the dark corners
of the palace.

When the queen took him on her travels,
all the people of the land rejoiced
at the sight of him.

"Here comes Prince Solatio!"
they would shout. "Prince Sunshine!
Ah, how much like his dead father
he is!"

His tutors were proud of him, too,
for he learned his lessons quickly.

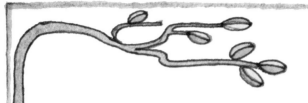

He could sing, he could dance,
and he learned to speak well
to great groups of people.

"He will surely make a fine king,"
his mother said.

Only his old nurse, Maga Rosa,
who had been the queen's nurse, too,
noticed an unusual thing
about the boy.
Nightly, she would find him
sitting at his window
staring at the sky.

"Is there a way to go to the moon?"
he would ask.

The years went by,
and as the prince approached
his nineteenth birthday, the queen
decided the time had come
to find a suitable wife
for her son.

"Only if she loves me,
and I love her, too,"
said the prince to his mother.

"Of course," answered the queen.

"You will know her
when you meet her," whispered Maga Rosa.

So a large celebration was held.
Princesses from far and near
were asked to attend —
princesses from neighboring lands
and far away from Naples and Sicily.

One by one, the princesses
were presented to the prince.

"Beautiful, but it is not her,"
the prince said to himself.
And of another even more beautiful,
"No, she is not the one."

The prince danced
with all the princesses.
He sat with them
and watched the entertainment.
And everyone at the court
watched and waited.

Although the prince was pleasant
and friendly enough, it became clear
that none of the beautiful princesses
captured his heart.

Toward the end of the evening,
he wandered out into the
garden for some air.

The full moon filled the sky,
and the very air seemed thick
with its light.
Suddenly,
the prince saw her before him—
the princess of his heart!

He reached out to touch her,
but his hand touched nothing.
Then,
his ears filled with a buzzing sound,
his head grew light,
and his heart felt as though
it had been pulled from his chest.
The prince uttered a long
and pitiful cry!

His eyes burned,
and he walked as if blind
as he stumbled back
into the great hall.

Whispers filled the room.
"What is wrong with the prince?"
He spun around, reaching out
as if trying to hold onto something.
Then he fell to the floor.

"The prince has been taken ill!"
cried the guests as the queen rushed
to her son.

"Don't touch him, my lady,"
Maga Rosa warned the queen.
"He has had a vision!"

Maga Rosa knelt by the prince
and crooned soft words until his eyes
fluttered open. She helped him to his
feet, then led him from the hall
as the guests looked on.

For two days and nights
the prince lay ill.
He tossed and turned and knew no one.
He called out,
"Luna, la luna — the moon, the moon!"

On the third day,
he seemed more himself,
and Maga Rosa brought his mother
to see him.

"I have found her, Mother,"
the prince said immediately.
"But, pity me
for I can never have her."
And the prince described
the beautiful princess he had seen
in the moonlight.

"We will search for her.
Send out messengers—"
the queen began to order.
But Maga Rosa put her hand
on the queen's arm.
"It is no use, my lady," she said.
"She is not of this world."

"The moon," the prince cried.
"She lives on the MOON...."

Slowly, the prince regained
his strength, but from that time on
he had only one interest.

He would sleep all day,
and when the sun had set,
he would awake and dress.
Then he would walk to the foothills
to sit and gaze at the moon.

The people began to call him
Prince "Pazzo," which means
"moonstruck."

"The poor prince has lost his mind,"
they would say. They made fun of him,
and he became the object of jokes.

When the moon was only a sliver,
the people would laugh and say,
"Prince Pazzo will be sad tonight."

Just as they had loved him before,
they now began to fear him.

"Who will rule
when the dear queen dies?" they asked.

As for the queen,
she thought her heart would break.

One night, as he sat in the
foothills of the dark mountains,
Prince Pazzo thought he heard singing.

"Wandering, wandering,
    night and day.
Where shall we live,
    where can we stay?
Driven from our homes
    by fearful men,
When may we ever stop
    and rest again?"

He caught sight of a band of the
strangest-looking little men he had
ever seen, apparently carrying all
their worldly goods upon their backs.

"Who are you?"
called out the prince.

The little men stopped,
frozen in fear.
After a moment
their leader came forward.

"Ah, good *signorino,*" he said,
"we are the Salvani —
protectors of all that is nature.
We were driven long ago from our
ancient homes by men who wished
to use the wilds for their selfish
purposes alone. Now we are wandering
to find another forest —
a new home.
But whenever we stop and the people
see us, they are frightened —
because we are different.
We are often forced to flee
for our lives.
We had hoped to find a place
in these somber mountains.
But, good *signorino,* do not harm us.
We will move on."

"I had no thought of harming you,"
answered the prince.

He paused.
"I too know what it is to be feared.
Even though I am a prince,
my people fear me greatly.
I have not become what they
expected me to be. Sometimes I
think they would feel easier if I
were to go away . . . forever."

"Poor *signorino.*
Is there anything we can do for you?"
asked the small leader.

"Thank you. I know of nothing.
But you are kind and generous
to offer," said the prince.
"Perhaps there is something
I can do for you."

"We ask very little,"
the leader of the Salvani answered.
"A quiet place, to ourselves,
where we may lead our simple lives
in peace."

"I shall ask my mother, the queen,
to grant you a place of your choice
here in the mountains.
Meanwhile, rest here for the night.
Tomorrow, I shall bring you an answer,"
said Prince Pazzo.
"But now, I must watch the moon."

"Watch the moon?" the Salvani asked.
"Please, why must you watch the moon?"

Prince Pazzo told the Salvani
about his vision.
"I would give everything I own
to visit the moon to see
if my love is really there."

"Ah, yes,"
said the leader of the Salvani.
"Well, do not let us keep you.
We will settle here and
await your answer."

The next day Prince Pazzo went
to his mother's rooms. She was
overjoyed to see her son
up and about during daylight hours.
When he asked if the Salvani
could settle in the mountains,
she gave her permission at once.
"Ah," she thought to herself,
"at least he is thinking of something
besides the moon."

The Salvani were very happy
to have a home once more.
They thanked the prince,
and then the leader said,
"Good prince,
perhaps we can help you, too.
There is a way to go to the moon."

"Tell me!" cried the prince.

"When next the moon is full,
you must go to the highest peak
carrying the most perfect rose
you can find," the leader said.

"When you arrive at the peak,
you will see two men who descend
with the light of every full moon
to observe the ways of earth.
Tell them you have a gift for
the moon-king's youngest daughter
and show them the rose.
If they say to leave the gift,
that they will deliver it,
tell them politely that you are
a prince and must present the rose
to the princess yourself.

"The rose, you see, will capture
her heart, for her greatest joy
is her garden.
Nothing pleases her more than
flowers she has never seen before,
and nothing pleases the moon-king
more than his youngest daughter's
happiness.

"But take care!
The moon's light is so intense
that if you stay too long,
you will go blind from its brightness.

"These magic spectacles
will help for a while.
But make your visit a short one.
Buona fortuna and *buon viaggio*."

The prince was overcome with joy.
He counted the days
until the moon became full. He was
even heard singing in the palace.

When the night of the full moon arrived,
he went to his mother to tell her
of his journey.

The poor queen wept,
believing her son had gone quite mad.

Maga Rosa comforted her.
"The mysteries
of this life and universe
are great, my lady.
Have faith."

The queen sighed
and went to select the royal garden's
most perfect rose.
She gave it to the prince.

"Shall I ever see you again?"
she asked. Receiving no answer,
she kissed him
and gave him her blessing.
She watched in tears
as the prince walked off into
the night.

Prince Pazzo
climbed the mountain to the peak
as the Salvani had instructed.
Sure enough, everything happened
as they said it would.

At last, the prince
was on the moon.

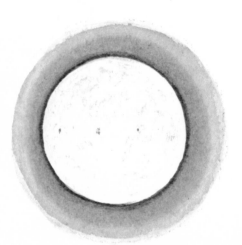

Prince Pazzo was received
as an honored guest by the moon-king.
A royal banquet was held,
and, one by one,
Prince Pazzo met the princesses
of the moon.

When the youngest, Lucia,
entered the hall,
Prince Pazzo caught his breath.
She *was* the princess of his heart!
He handed her the perfect rose.

"Oh, Father, look!" Lucia cried.
"Isn't it beautiful?
Thank you, earth-prince, for the
strangest and most beautiful flower
I have ever seen.
Please, tell me about your earth."

And they sat together talking
for the evening. She confided that
the two earth-observers
once described the prince to her.
That is why she had visited his garden
to catch a glimpse of him.
She added that she had patiently hoped
the prince would find his way
to the moon.

When the end of the evening came,
it was obvious to all
that Prince Pazzo and Princess Lucia
were in love.

Prince Pazzo easily won the hearts
of the kingdom, and the moon-king
was especially pleased
to see his daughter's happiness.

Days pass quickly for those in love.

But, one morning when the prince awoke,
his eyes burned fiercely and tears
ran down his cheeks. He remembered
the warning of the Salvani.
He was going blind
from the brightness of the moon.
The magic spectacles no longer
protected him.

With great sadness,
the moon-doctors announced that only
the prince's return to the earth
would save his sight.

The prince would not consider it.
"I would rather be blind than
be separated from my love,"
he declared.

Lucia would not hear of it.

"I could never spend a happy day
knowing that it was I
who made you blind.
But, why be separated?"
the princess asked.
"I shall return to earth with you."

The moon-king made the arrangements
for their departure.

"I will miss you, my Lucia," he said,
"but your happiness means more to me."

On earth,
the queen was overjoyed at the return
of her son. She immediately took
Princess Lucia to her heart.

Within a few days,
the prince's sight was restored,
and a week-long celebration was held.

On the last day the wedding
of Prince Pazzo of the Dolomites
and Princess Lucia of the Moon
took place with great joy.

The earth fascinated the princess
as the moon had the prince,
and she quickly captured
the love of everyone.

"How grateful we are for our
prince and princess. What a fine
king and queen they will someday be,"
the people said.

But as time passed, it was
noticed by all that the princess
was growing paler.
She was often heard to sigh
and to complain of a heaviness
around her heart.
Prince Pazzo noted too
that she laughed less and less.

It was the mountains
that bothered her the most, she said —
the tall, dark mountains
that kept even the sun from the land.

At night, she could not sleep.
She would sit for hours and gaze
at the moon.
She would cry out in fear
of the darkness.
Candles and lanterns were brought
to surround her, even during the day.

In spite of every effort,
she continued to grow thin, pale,
and listless.

The prince was desperate.

"My dearest wife," he said.
"We shall return
to the moon. It is our only hope.
I would rather be blind than have
eyes to see you suffer so."

But the princess would not hear of it
and begged him to wait a while.
Surely she would soon grow well,
she said.
The prince filled her room
with flowers, hoping they would help.
They did not.

The joy of the kingdom
was hushed.

The princess grew worse,
day by night,
until at last the doctors
announced that nothing could be done.
Princess Lucia was dying.

Prince Pazzo closed the door to their rooms.
Standing at the window,
he thought he saw Maga Rosa,
riding a horse into the dark night
under the crescent moon.

Some nights later, when the
moon had reached its full light,
the queen heard a tapping
at her balcony door.
Opening it, she stepped back
in fright at what she saw.
A group of strange small men
pressed toward her.

"My lady," said one. "Please do
not be afraid. We have come to help,
not to harm."

It was the leader of the Salvani
who spoke.
"You have been generous
and kind to us.

"We have come to repay our debt.
I beg you to trust us and wait."
Turning to the Salvani, he said,
"Come, friends, we have work to do
and not much time."

Then they disappeared
over the balcony's edge.

"You called, my lady?"
asked Maga Rosa,
who had been watching from the door.

"They said they would help,
those strange small men,"
answered the queen as if in a daze.
"All we can do is trust and wait."

The full moon climbed higher
in the sky. Suddenly,
from the distant mountaintops
faint singing could be heard.

> "Twist the beams,
>   twist the rays,
> Weave the strongest
>   ropes of light.
> Give the lovers
>   happy days.
> Pray our magic works
>   tonight."

It was the Salvani.
They had climbed to the tops
of the tallest peaks.

Gathering the moonbeams
falling from the sky,
they twisted them
into great bright ropes.
Soon the light from the ropes
was bright as the moon itself.

Then they wove the ropes
into shining nets of moonbeams
and cast them over the dark peaks.

As the light poured down the mountains, the black shapes changed to glimmering white, blue, pink, and yellow.

One after the other,
the mountains were transformed.

The queen watched in wonder.
Then, followed by Maga Rosa, she ran through the hallways to the rooms of the prince and princess.

"Look, my children," she cried.
"A miracle is happening."

Princess Lucia drew herself up.
When she saw the glittering sight, her face flushed, and she smiled and called to Prince Pazzo.

"My love," she said weakly.
"The light. It is like my home.
I can feel it flowing in my veins."

And when the full moon set,
the mountains still glowed.

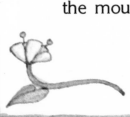

As the sun began to warm the sky,
Maga Rosa said softly,
"Ecco fatto — it is finished."
The Dolomite mountains shimmered
even more.

The sun reflected off them
and filled the land.
What once was dark and dismal
had become a place
of light and brightness.

It was not long before
the princess recovered.
The people rejoiced and told
many stories about the mountains
and how and why they had changed.

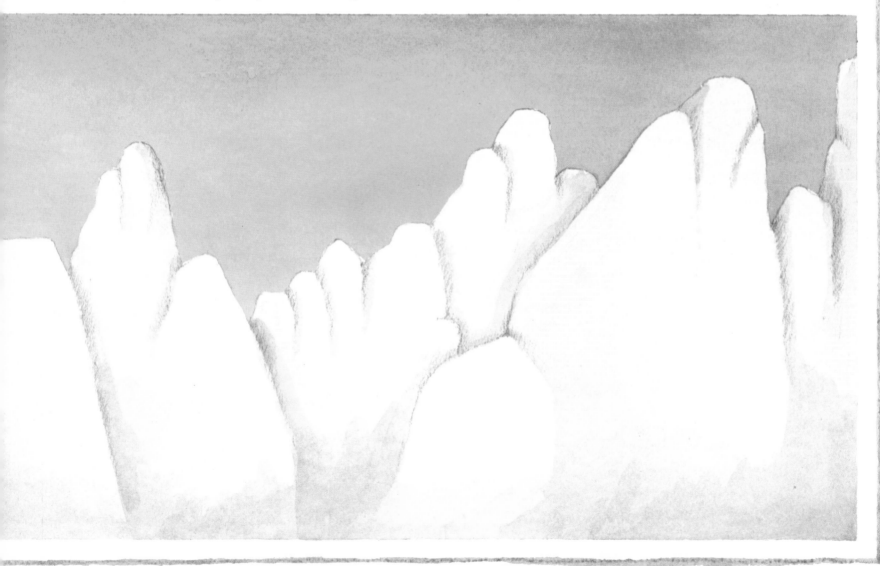

Years later,
the good queen passed the kingdom over
to Prince Pazzo and Princess Lucia,
who ruled wisely and well.
They lived a long, happy life
and had many children.

And Maga Rosa, though very old,
insisted on being their nurse.

Old Uncle Storyteller paused.

"Oh, Zio," the children said, "that's not really true, is it?"

"Indeed it is," said Zio Narratore. "Just look at our Dolomites.
Have they ever lost their 'moon-light'?
And another thing. When the moon-king came to earth
to visit his grandchildren,
he brought them a special flower from their mother's old garden.
They planted it atop the Dolomite peaks to honor the Salvani.
Today the mountains are covered with its lovely blooms."

Zio Narratore picked up his knapsack and smiled.

"We call that flower *stella alpina* — edelweiss."

"*Ciao, ragazzini.*"

"*Ciao*, Zio," called the children. "Come back soon."

Zio Narratore waved and trudged down the road
to another village
to tell other stories to other children.

This book was set in 14 Pt. VIP Korinna by Publishers Phototype, Inc.
It was printed by offset on 80 lb. Patina supplied by Lindenmeyer Paper Corporation.

The drawings were done in colored inks and watercolor
on Schoellers 140 lb. 100% rag watercolor paper.

Separations were made by Capper Incorporated.

Printed by Pearl Pressman Liberty.
Bound by Economy Book Bindery.